the UnDeRDOgS

WE'RE NOT THE CHAMPIONS

TEAM UNDERDOG

By Tracey West

ILLUSTRATED BY Kyla May

SCHOLASTIC INC.

Copyright © 2022 by Scholastic Inc.

All rights reserved. Published by Scholastic Inc., *Publishers since 1920.* SCHOLASTIC and associated logos are trademarks and/or registered trademarks of Scholastic Inc.

The publisher does not have any control over and does not assume any responsibility for author or third-party websites or their content.

No part of this publication may be reproduced, stored in a retrieval system, or transmitted in any form or by any means, electronic, mechanical, photocopying, recording, or otherwise, without written permission of the publisher. For information regarding permission, write to Scholastic Inc., Attention: Permissions Department, 557 Broadway, New York, NY 10012.

This book is a work of fiction. Names, characters, places, and incidents are either the product of the author's imagination or are used fictitiously, and any resemblance to actual persons, living or dead, business establishments, events, or locales is entirely coincidental.

Library of Congress Catologing-in-Publication Data available

ISBN 978-1-338-73273-3

10 9 8 7 6 5 4 3 2   22 23 24 25 26
Printed in Italy   183

First printing 2022
Book design by Jessica Meltzer

For Bollie, who's as funny
as a Boston terrier and as gorgeous
as a poodle. —T. W.

I dedicate this book to my
#1 fans, my nephew Will and my
niece Erin. xoxo —K. M.

Table of Contents

MEET THE UNDERDOGS

THE BEST OF BARKSDALE

1. SCAREDY-DOG 1

2. MEGA SPLASH! 13

3. ICE CREAM FIGHT 23

4. DINNER WITH COCO 33

5. ZEE BEST OF ZEE BEST 45

6. RIBBIT! 65

7. COOL IS COOL 79

8. GIVE ME A "B"! 89

9. ALL FUN AND GAMES? 105

10. BOWWOW, BARKSDALE! 111

11. TRIPPING AND SLIPPING 123

12. SPLASHING AND CRASHING 133

13. SPLAT! 141

14. LOYALTY 153

CHAPTER 1

SCAREDY-DOG

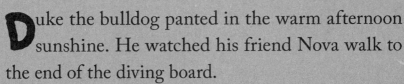

Duke the bulldog panted in the warm afternoon sunshine. He watched his friend Nova walk to the end of the diving board.

"I call this move the Butterfly!" she announced, jumping up and down.

She bounced off. **BOING!** She launched into the air, flapping her front legs.

Whoa, that looks scary! Duke thought.

Nova landed in the lake. Water droplets shot up as she hit the water. Then she swam to shore and climbed onto the grass, shaking her golden-yellow fur.

"Be careful, Nova!" cried Peanut. The little dog was stretched out on a beach towel next to Duke. "I don't want to get my fur wet!"

"You don't know what you're missing!" Nova replied, and she shook her head again, hitting Peanut with one last sprinkle of water.

"Aaaargh!" Peanut cried.

Duke laughed. "It's just water, Peanut."

"Oh yeah?" Peanut asked. "Why don't you jump in, then?"

Duke frowned. Peanut knew why Duke wouldn't jump in. He wasn't afraid of water. But heights—yikes!

"Hey, look at me!" Harley called from the diving board. "I call this one the Flipperoo!"

Harley launched off the board using her short, powerful legs. She somersaulted in the air.

SPLASH! She slammed into the water. Then her head popped up.

"What do you think of that one?" she asked as she doggy-paddled to the shore.

"I liked it," Nova replied, and she bounded toward the diving board. "I want to try it!"

Harley shook the water off her fur, and Peanut frowned.

"I keep getting wet!" he complained.

"Well, maybe you shouldn't have come to the lake, then," Duke teased.

Peanut leaned back and slid his sunglasses over his eyes. "It's Saturday! Lake Barksdale is the place to be."

Duke gazed around. Sunlight glittered on the dark blue surface of the lake. On one side was a sandy beach, and on the other side, a grassy meadow. Dogs swam in the water, dug in the sand, played volleyball on the shore, and snacked at picnic tables. The welcome sign informed visitors that Lake Barksdale was:

THE BEST LAKE FOR SWIMMING!
THE BEST LAKE FOR PICNICKING!
THE BEST LAKE FOR HAVING FUN!

Typical, Duke thought. *Everyone and everything in Barksdale wants to be the best. And everyone and everything in Barksdale is* the best. *Everyone except us.*

Duke, Peanut, Nova, and Harley were four friends known as the Underdogs. They weren't the best at anything. Except, maybe, at being themselves. And that was just fine with Duke.

Nova tried to somersault off the diving board. But instead of curling her body into a ball, like Harley had, her legs spread out in all different directions. She landed on the water with a **SPLAT** instead of a **SPLASH!**

She ran out of the water, laughing. "I'm going to need some practice," she said. "Hey, Duke, you wanna try the diving board?"

"I think I'll just dip my paws in the water," Duke replied.

"Aw, come on, it's not even that high," Nova urged.

Duke didn't answer right away. Nova had recently tried to help him get over his fear of heights—one of the many things he was afraid of. It hadn't worked, but Duke had been proud of himself for trying.

"*Weeellllll*," he said slowly, "it *is* hot. And jumping in would cool me down."

Harley pulled Duke off his blanket. "You don't have to do anything fancy. I'll give you a push if you want."

"No, you definitely don't have to push me," Duke said, suddenly feeling nervous. But he followed Harley and Nova up to the diving board on the end of the dock.

Harley took off. **"THE ROCKET!"** she yelled. She bounced on the end of the board once . . . twice . . . and the third time, she shot straight up into the air. Then she landed in the water back paws first, with her front legs down at her sides.

Nova giggled. **"THE JELLYFISH!"** Nova called out, charging off the board. She wiggled her legs in a silly way as she sailed across the water.

The two pups paddled in the water, waiting for Duke.

"Come on, Duke!" Nova shouted.

"You can do it!" Harley yelled.

Duke slowly walked to the edge of the board. He looked down into the deep lake. His heart began to beat fast, and he froze.

"Nope," he said. "Just nope. I thought I could do it, but I can't."

"That's okay, Duke!" Nova told him.

Duke walked back to the ladder. He frowned to see two familiar pups waiting there.

It was Mandy and Randy Fetcherton. They were twins with floppy ears—and bad attitudes.

"What's the matter, Duke? Scared?" Mandy asked.

Randy pointed. "He's a scaredy-dog!"

They started laughing, and some of the other dogs on the beach joined in.

CHAPTER 2

MEGA SPLASH!

Duke wished he could become invisible. Randy and Mandy were so mean! And he couldn't even walk away. They were blocking his path.

Suddenly, something small streaked past him onto the diving board.

"CANNONBALL!"

Duke couldn't believe his eyes. It was Peanut! The little dog sprang from the end of the diving board, jumping impossibly far. Then he crashed down into the lake.

MEGA SPLASH! Water sprayed up, drenching Duke as well as Mandy and Randy. Peanut's head emerged from the water.

"Hmpf!" Mandy huffed.

"Whatever," Randy grumbled.

The soggy twins slunk away, and Duke gratefully trotted back to his blanket. Peanut ran out of the water.

"Towel! Towel!" he cried, and Duke quickly handed one to his friend.

"My fur is going to be a mess after this," Peanut grumbled.

"That was really nice of you to do that, dude," Duke said.

The little dog shrugged. "Nobody messes with my best buddy!"

Nova and Harley came out of the lake, too.

"Mandy and Randy are **THE WORST!**" Harley complained. "They're always giving us a hard time."

Nova gazed off into the distance, as though she were imagining something. "Don't worry. We're going to keep doing better at our K-9 exams. Then they won't be able to tease us anymore!"

The four friends went to Barksdale Academy. Each year, they formed teams and took nine K-9 exams. Duke, Peanut, Nova, and Harley had always failed. But this year, things were starting to look different. Thinking about it, Duke had a . . .

The K-1 exam tested the dogs on agility. The teams had to race through an obstacle course. The four friends had never been able to finish the course in the past.

But this time, thanks to Nova, they had tried something new.

Duke had walked around the tall ramp instead of trying to climb it.

Peanut had worn a special suit so he wouldn't get messy.

Harley had stayed focused thanks to a fake squirrel.

And Nova had zoomed around the course perfectly—until she crashed into the judges' table at the end.

The friends had adapted the test to make it work for them, and they'd passed by one point. They'd also earned a new team name: **THE UNDERDOGS.**

"Duke, are you thinking about the agility test again?" Peanut asked, poking him.

Duke snapped out of the flashback. "Yeah. I still can't believe we passed."

"And we'll pass the K-2 exam, too," Nova said confidently. "Although I wish I knew exactly how we were going to be tested."

TING-A-LING-A-LING!

Harley's ears perked up. "Let's not worry about that now. The Top Cone truck is here. It's ice cream time!"

Duke's tummy rumbled. "Sounds good to me!"

The Underdogs trotted toward the picnic area, following the sound of the ice cream truck's bells.

Then they heard something different.

Harley's ears twitched again. She frowned. "That's not the Top Cone bell."

Suddenly, they heard shouts coming from the picnic area.

"Uh-oh!" Duke said. "Sounds like trouble!"

TOP CONE

BEST CONE

22

CHaPTeR 3

ICE CREAM FIGHT

The Underdogs hurried to the picnic area, where two ice cream trucks were parked next to each other. Izzy, a tan curly-haired dog stood in front of the Top Cone truck. The other truck was decorated with colorful polka dots and had the words BEST CONE painted on the side in bright letters. A white dog with black spots stood in front of it.

"Beat it, Buster!" Izzy was saying to the black-and-white dog. "This is Top Cone territory."

"There's no law that says I can't sell here, too," Buster shot back.

Izzy frowned and turned to the crowd of pups waiting for frozen treats. "Get your ice cream here! We have the best vanilla in Barksdale!"

Nova turned to Duke, Peanut, and Harley. "Her vanilla *is* really yummy."

Buster stepped in front of Izzy. "Get your ice cream *here*! We have the best *banana* in Barksdale!"

Nova nodded. "He might be right. His banana is really good!"

Izzy grabbed a can of whipped cream. "Get your ice cream from Top Cone. We have the best whipped cream in Barksdale!"

She pressed the button. The whipped cream squirted right onto Buster's snout! Everyone laughed.

He glared and picked up a pink plastic bottle. "Oh yeah? Well, we have the *best* strawberry syrup."

Pssssshhhhhhhhht! He squirted it right into Izzy's face!

Everyone gasped.

"Uh-oh," Peanut said. "This is going to get messy . . ."

"**FOOD FIGHT!**" someone yelled, and Izzy and Buster couldn't control themselves. Ice cream ingredients flew back and forth across the air . . .

A barrage of bananas!

A shower of sprinkles!

A collection of cones!

A flurry of frozen foods!

CHOMP! CHOMP! CHOMP! Harley jumped in the air again and again, gulping down the ingredients as they flew through the air. Soon other dogs were copying her, chowing down on the flying treats.

Duke didn't jump. He preferred staying close to the ground. But it was fun to watch the others try to catch the food.

"I wish Coco could see this," he remarked.

Peanut cocked his head. "Coco your cousin? She's coming to visit tomorrow, right?"

Duke had only met his cousin Coco a few times. She and her family lived across the ocean, in France. But Duke's family sometimes video chatted with them. Coco talked with a fancy accent, and she was always perfectly groomed and wearing cute accessories. And now she was coming to Barksdale for a few weeks for a special exchange student program.

"Her plane from Paris lands tonight," Duke replied. "Tomorrow is when me, you, Nova, and Harley are taking her to Chef Wolfgang's Bistro for dinner, remember? This way she can get to know some other pups before her first day at school."

Nova and Harley bounded over.

"I don't think we're going to get any ice cream," Harley said sadly. "But I did manage to catch two bananas and a mouthful of sprinkles."

Nova sighed. "You know, sometimes it's not easy living in a town where everyone always wants to be the best."

"Yeah," Peanut agreed. "Duke, I hope your cousin doesn't have trouble fitting in here in Barksdale."

"I think Coco will fit in here just fine," Duke answered, but he actually wasn't so sure.

Duke hadn't told his friends how glamorous his cousin was. He'd been hoping that they would all just get along at dinner tomorrow night and that perfect Coco wouldn't notice how *im*perfect Duke and his friends were.

WHOMP! A banana hit him in the side of the head.

"Mine!" Harley shouted, and she bounced on the banana and gobbled it down.

Nova laughed. "Come on, pups. Let's go get some ice cream in town."

"Good plan!" Duke agreed.

32

chApter 4

VOTED
#1
SALON

WINNER OF THE
PRETTIEST PETALS
AWARD THREE
YEARS IN A ROW!

FIONA'S FLOWER SHOP
THE BEST BLOOMS IN BARKSDALE!

Bubbles
and Bows
We'll Help You Look
Your Barkin' BEST!

DINNER WITH COCO

"**T**his eez such a charming little town," remarked Duke's cousin Coco as they walked down Barksdale's Main Street.

"Thanks," Duke replied. He liked hearing Coco's sweet French accent, and she always had such nice things to say. But still, he felt a little nervous since she had arrived the night before. Why?

She's so perfect! Duke had thought. *Her white fur is clean and shiny. Her ears are cute and tiny. And she's so stylish!*

Coco had climbed off the plane wearing a pink scarf and smelling like fresh flowers. Duke still had sand in his paws from the lake, and he smelled like bananas from the food fight.

Tonight, he'd tried to spiff himself up before they went out to eat at Chef Wolfgang's Bistro. He'd taken a bath and blow-dried his fur, and even though he still smelled faintly of bananas, it was kind of nice.

Coco, of course, looked even better than she had the day before. She wore a sparkly necklace and a little pink cap on top of her head.

"I'm excited to meet your friends," she said as they walked toward the restaurant.

"They're the best," Duke said. "I really hope you—"

Nova bounded up to them, her tail wagging with excitement. For a second, it looked like she was going to plow right into Coco, but she skidded to a stop just in time. Duke sighed with relief.

"Coco! I mean you must be Coco, right? Duke's cousin? 'Cause who else would it be?" Nova was talking really fast. "I'm Duke's friend—not his best friend, that's Peanut over there, with Harley, who's *my* best friend, but when you really think about it, the four of us are all best friends, right? Who says four pups can't be best friends?"

"It eez nice to meet you," Coco said. "You must be Nova. Duke told me he had a friend with a lot of energy."

Nova grinned. "Yup, that's me! Come on, you've got to meet Harley and Peanut."

Nova ran off, and Duke and Coco caught up to her outside the bistro. Duke noticed that Peanut was wearing a yellow bow tie with red polka dots.

"I'm Peanut. Pleasure to meet you," the little dog said.

"I like your tie," Coco told him, and Peanut beamed.

Why didn't I think of wearing something fancy? Duke scolded himself.

Harley stepped in front of Peanut. "I'm Harley. Nice to meet you. Now let's go get some grub! I'm sooooooo hungry!"

Everything's going just fine, Duke thought as the five dogs walked through the doorway. Each restaurant in town claimed to be the best, but everyone knew that Chef Wolfgang's Bistro really *was* the best.

Duke's mouth watered as the smell of food hit his nose. A large droplet of drool started to fall from his lips, but he slurped it back up just in time.

A waiter showed them to a round table topped with a white tablecloth. Coco took a seat between Duke and Peanut. Coco picked up her menu and read it.

"The food here eez very interesting," she said.

Nova nodded. "It's awesome! You've got to try the peanut butter pasta. Or the peanut butter bacon burger. Or the pizza topped with pineapple and—"

"Peanut butter?" Coco finished.

Nova nodded. "Yes, how did you guess?"

"There eez peanut butter in everything," Coco replied.

"It's Chef Wolfgang's specialty," Peanut explained. Then he nodded to Coco. "Get a load of that Dalmatian over there. I bet his food is hitting the spot. Get it? Spot?"

"That eez funny, Peanut," Coco replied.

Peanut puffed up, pleased. "I've got lots more jokes. What do you call a dog that's been out in the cold?"

Coco shrugged. "I do not know."

A Pupsicle!

Peanut laughed so hard at his own joke he almost fell off his chair.

Coco giggled.

Wow, Coco even likes Peanut's corny jokes, Duke thought. *Maybe I had nothing to worry about after all.*

When their waiter came, everyone ordered the same thing—peanut butter pasta. Peanut started to tell more jokes, but Nova and Harley interrupted him, asking Coco questions about Paris.

Soon, the waiter came back with five bowls of pasta and placed one in front of each pup. Nova's tail wagged with anticipation, and Duke slurped up another drop of drool.

Duke cleared his throat. "Before we eat, I'd just like to say—"

"**MMMMM**, smells so good!" Harley cried, and she buried her snout in her food, sending sauce splashing onto Peanut's bow tie.

"Hey, my tie!" Peanut cried.

Nova leaned over the table and dipped her napkin into a glass of water.

"This'll get it right off!" Nova promised, and she reached for Peanut . . .

. . . planting her elbow on her pasta bowl and sending it flying up, up, up into the air.

Duke stared, frozen, as the bowl came down, down, down . . . and landed with a splat—right on Coco's head!

ZEE BEST OF
ZEE BEST

Nova, Harley, and Peanut all stared at Coco with wide eyes, waiting to see her reaction.

Coco stuck out her tongue and snagged a strand of spaghetti dangling from the top of her head. Then she slurped it down.

"Eet eez very good!" she said, and then she smiled.

Everyone laughed with relief, and Duke beamed at his cousin.

Coco might be much cooler than we are, but at least she has a good sense of humor, Duke thought.

Unfortunately, the waiter did *not* have a good sense of humor. He frowned when he saw the mess at their table. Nova grabbed a towel from him and started to clean up the spilled pasta, but that caused her to knock over a glass of water, which made everything a little messier. But they eventually got everything cleaned up. And they all had Chef Wolfgang's famous peanut butter pie for dessert.

"Your friends are very nice," Coco remarked as she and Duke walked home afterward.

Duke beamed. "Yeah, I think they're great," he said.

"I am looking forward to going to school tomorrow and meeting the rest of your classmates," Coco added.

"Mmm-hmm," Duke replied. But he was starting to feel a little nervous again.

Duke hadn't told Coco that he and his friends weren't the best, like everyone else in Barksdale. Or that, in fact, the Underdogs were the *worst* students in the whole school. He knew she would find out sooner or later. But he wanted it to be later. *Much* later. And once Coco saw them around all the other perfect pups at Barksdale . . .

Don't worry, Duke, he told himself. *Coco likes us! Nothing's going to change that—right?*

The next morning, Duke and Coco met Nova, Harley, and Peanut on the corner of Bark Avenue so they could walk to school together. Nova ran circles around everyone.

"It's your first day of school at Barksdale Academy, Coco! How exciting!" she said.

"And you're looking pretty snazzy, too," Peanut added.

The French bulldog carried a pink backpack with sparkly jewels on it and wore a cool and chunky necklace.

"Thank you," Coco replied. "And yes, I am excited. We know all about zee Barksdale Academy in France. It is one of zee best schools in zee whole world! And zee students are **ZEE BEST OF ZEE BEST**."

"Well, not *all* the students," Harley began. "Actually, we're—"

"Squirrel!" Duke cried, and Harley stopped. Her head swung from right to left. Then she shot off toward a tree.

That was close, Duke thought. *Harley almost told Coco that we're underdogs!*

Harley came bounding back a couple minutes later, panting. "I think the squirrels around here are getting faster," she said.

"Oh, but you are very fast, Harley," Coco remarked, and Harley grinned.

Just then, Mandy and Randy walked up, and Duke froze. Those two were nothing but trouble.

The twins stopped and looked Coco up and down, their heads moving at the same time.

"You must be the new exchange student," Mandy said.

"Yeah, you must be Coco," Randy added.

Coco smiled. "Yes, how did you know?"

"Well, for starters, you don't look like anyone else around here," Mandy remarked.

"Nobody else," Randy echoed.

Mandy continued. "Anyway, it looks like you've accidentally run into the biggest losers in the school, so—"

"This is my cousin, Duke, and our friends," Coco interrupted, frowning. "What do you mean, 'losers'?"

Mandy's eyes widened. "You're Duke's cousin? **you?**"

Duke took a deep breath and looked Mandy in the eyes. "Yes, she is."

"Do you have a problem with that?" Peanut asked, scooting between Duke and Mandy.

"No, I'm just surprised," Mandy replied. "See you in class, Underdogs."

Mandy and Randy turned up their snouts and then trotted toward the school.

"Underdogs? What did she mean, 'Underdogs'?" Coco asked.

Oh no! Duke thought. *Coco's going to find out what a mess we are! I need more time to show her my good qualities. Like how I'm a good friend. And how I'm strong. And how I can stuff thirty-six biscuits into my mouth at once . . .*

Nova spoke up. "It's our team name," she explained. "Duke, Harley, Peanut, and I compete together in the school's K-9 exams. We call ourselves the Underdogs, because—"

"We're here!" Duke announced, glad that they had reached the front steps of the school. They walked inside, where students were chatting on the way to their first class of the day.

Barksdale Academy

Duke and his friends made their way through the main hall, filled with glass cases that held dozens and dozens of gleaming trophies. They made a right after the gym, and walked toward a door marked B-3. A small dog with long fur greeted them as they entered.

"Hello, Coco!" she said. "I am Principal Finella Finefur. Welcome to Barksdale Academy."

"I am so happy to be here," Coco replied.

"And we are happy to have you," the principal said. "Please take the desk next to Ollie."

She motioned to a dog with wheels strapped to his back legs. Coco trotted over to her desk and smiled at Ollie.

"Cool wheels," she said.

Ollie grinned at her. "Thanks!"

Principal Finefur adjusted her glasses and clapped her paws. "Take your seats, everyone! We have a lot to cover today."

Duke sat at his desk by the window, next to Peanut. Principal Finefur addressed the class.

"As all of you know, Ace Swiftrunner, our top student here at Barksdale, is at La Paluche d'Or School in Paris for a month, and we have their top student, Coco Parfait, in exchange," she explained. "And Coco just happens to be Duke's cousin!"

Duke saw Mandy and Randy roll their eyes at each other.

"Coco is here just in time to compete in our K-2 exam," the principal continued. "She will take Ace's place on Team Awesome along with Mandy, Randy, and Ollie."

Duke gasped. *Coco, on Team Awesome? Oh no!*

"Yes!" Ollie cheered, and Mandy and Randy smiled smugly. Duke frowned. He'd been hoping that Coco would be on Team Underdog with him and his friends. But it made sense for her to join Team Awesome in Ace's place.

Coco raised her paw. "What is zee K-2 exam?"

"The K-2 exam is a loyalty test," Principal Finefur replied. "Next week is our annual Field Day competition against the Pawston School for Canine Excellence. During that event, we will test our students' loyalty by judging them on their school spirit and their overall performance in the Field Day activities."

"And how is theez a test of loyalty?" Coco asked.

"A strong display of school spirit and teamwork shows loyalty to Barksdale!" said Principal Finefur. "Now, who can tell me about the history of the Barksdale and Pawston Field Day event?"

A small dog with feathery ears raised her paw. "Ooh, ooh, I know something!"

Principal Finefur nodded. "Yes, Athena?"

61

"The event began fifty-three years ago, to settle a debate over which school was the best," Athena said. "Barksdale has never lost to Pawston once! So statistically, that means we have a very good chance of winning."

"Yes, we do," Principal Finefur agreed. "But we must not take that for granted. I expect every Barksdale student to do their very best, and more. Now then, let's talk about that first Field Day . . ."

After her long lecture, the bell rang.

"Our next class is just down the hall," Duke told Coco as they made their way to the door.

Randy and Mandy blocked their way.

"Coco, you should sit with us at lunch," Mandy said.

"Yeah, at lunch," Randy echoed.

"Coco's going to sit with me and my friends," Duke said. "My mom packed a special lunch for us."

Coco nodded. "I will sit with my cousin, but thank you for zee invitation."

Mandy sniffed. "Do what you want," she said. "But when you change your mind, we'll be waiting for you."

"Yeah," Randy said.

The twins turned up their snouts and walked away.

Duke turned to Coco. "I'm glad you're going to eat with us."

"Of course, Duke," she replied. "You are my family. And your friends are very nice."

Duke smiled, relieved. *Even though Coco has to be on Team Awesome for the K–2 exam, at least she still wants to hang out with us!*

CHAPTER 6

RIBBIT!

Students swarmed Coco as she and Duke walked down the hallway.

"Coco, what's it like in France?"

"Coco, where did you get that necklace?"

"Coco, say something in your cute accent!"

"Coco!"

"Coco!"

"COCO!"

The pups who couldn't get close to Coco asked Duke questions instead.

"Is Coco really your cousin?"

"What's Coco like at home?"

"Can you bring Coco to the lake this weekend?"

Is this what it's like to be popular? Duke wondered. Then the bell rang, and everyone scrambled to get to class.

By the time lunchtime came, just about every pup at Barksdale Academy had asked Coco to sit with them. Duke swaggered a little as he entered the cafeteria with his popular cousin. All eyes were on them!

They sat down at a table with Nova, Harley, and Peanut. Duke opened the lunch bag his mom had packed for him and Coco. Inside was a skinny loaf of bread and a wedge of stinky cheese.

Peanut sniffed the air. "What are you having for lunch? An old shoe covered in garbage gravy?"

"It's cheese, from France," Duke replied. "Mom doesn't want Coco to feel homesick."

Peanut stuck out his tongue. "Blech!"

Coco laughed. "It eez very nice cheese," she said. "You should try some."

"No, thanks," Peanut replied. "I'll stick with my sandwich." He held up a neat peanut butter sandwich with the crusts cut off.

"Well, I think your cheese smells yummy," Harley said.

"Would you and Nova like to try some?" Coco asked.

Nova held up a thermos. "Sure, and then you can try some of Granny Goldenfur's soup. She makes it with—"

"What eez 'ribbit'?" Coco asked.

"I didn't say that," Nova replied. "I think—"

RIBBIT!

Harley sat straight up. Her ears stood at attention. Her nose twitched.

"That's a frog!" she cried. Then she ducked under the table. "There's a frog under here!"

"A frog?" Duke asked. Frogs were pretty high on the list of things Duke was afraid of. Along with heights, of course. And spiders. And snakes. And loud noises. And lightning. And clowns. And . . .

RIBBIT!

A small green frog hopped onto the table, right in front of Duke's snout!

"FROG!" Duke yelled, and he jumped up onto the lunch table!

The table rocked back and forth, and everyone's food slid onto the floor. Nova, Peanut, Harley, and Coco jumped out of their seats, too.

"SOMEBODY STOP IT BEFORE IT HOPS ON ME!" Duke shouted.

"I can't move! My paws are stuck in the stinky cheese!" Peanut wailed.

"ON IT!" Harley cried, and she lunged for the frog. It jumped away, and Harley chased after it.

RIBBIT!

The frog kept jumping, and Harley kept chasing after it, knocking down cafeteria chairs as she raced by. All the pups in the cafeteria began laughing and pointing.

The frog finally stopped on the floor in front of their friend Athena. The quick-thinking canine scooped up the frog in an empty juice cup.

"I've got you now, little guy," she said. "How did you escape from the nature lab? Let's get you back there."

"I almost had it!" Harley cried, and bounded back to the Underdogs' table.

Duke, still frozen, stared at the mess of food under his paws and on the floor. Then he heard Mandy's mocking voice ring through the lunchroom.

"Look at Duke the scaredy-dog! Afraid of a frog!" she said.

"Scaredy-dog! Afraid of a frog!" Randy chanted.

Everyone laughed as Duke slowly climbed down from the table and slid into his seat. Coco stared at him, wide-eyed.

Mandy and Randy marched up to their table.

"Coco, this table is a bit of a mess," Mandy remarked.

"Are you sure you don't want to sit with us?" Randy asked. "We can share our lunch with you."

Coco looked down at the bread and the stinky cheese, which had Peanut's paw prints all over it.

"Thank you, I think I will sit with you," she said, and she started to gather her things.

"Don't leave, Coco," Duke said. He picked up the cheese sandwich and brushed it off. "See, it's not so bad."

"That eez very nice of you, Duke. But I think I should get to know my new teammates anyway, right?" She started to walk away, and Mandy and Randy turned and stuck their tongues out at Duke.

"Those rotten rats!" Peanut cried. "I bet they're the ones who put that frog under the table, just to make you look bad, Duke. They know you're afraid of everything."

Duke sighed. "Well, if that was their plan, it worked. Coco is sitting at their table. And I've ruined everyone's lunch!"

"It's okay," Nova said, picking up her thermos, which had survived the whole frog incident. "There's enough of Granny's soup for all of us!"

"Thanks, Nova," Peanut and Harley said. Duke gazed over at Coco, who was now sitting with Mandy, Randy, and Ollie. They were talking and laughing, like nothing had happened.

Are they laughing at me? Duke wondered, and he sighed. He couldn't blame Coco for sitting at another table after the big mess he had made.

Still . . . it hurt just a teeny little bit.

CHAPTER 7

COCO IS COOL

When school ended, Duke moped down the side-walk behind Coco, who walked ahead of him with Mandy, Randy, and several other students.

Peanut trotted up to his friend. "What's the matter, dude? You look sadder than a hound who just finished his bone."

"It's Coco," Duke replied. "I was worried that she was too cool for us, and I guess I was right. She never would have gone off with Mandy and Randy if I hadn't jumped on top of that table like a big scaredy-dog."

Peanut shrugged. "It would have happened eventually," he said. "I mean, look at her. She *is* cooler than us."

He stopped and paused dramatically. "Let her go, Duke. You can't stop a shooting star from flying across the galaxy."

"I guess not," Duke said with a sigh. They had reached Duke's house. Coco waved to her new friends and gracefully climbed up the steps and went inside.

"See you tomorrow, Peanut," Duke said.

Peanut nodded. "Catch you on the pup side!"

"Duke, Coco, how was school?" Duke's mom called from the kitchen.

Coco stopped to chat with his mom, but Duke didn't answer. He went straight upstairs to his room.

Duke's bedroom was his favorite place in Barksdale. He had a big, comfy bed with blankets he could pull over his head when he was feeling scared at night, and

seven night-lights plugged in so he wouldn't be afraid of the dark.

Duke sat on the bed and picked up a scruffy stuffed green duck. He gave it a squeeze.

"It happened, Mr. Quacky," Duke told his favorite stuffed animal. "Coco knows I'm not cool."

There was a knock on the door, and his cousin peeked in his room.

"Duke, your mother has a snack for us," she said.

"I'm not hungry," Duke replied.

"I will tell her," Coco said, and as she turned to leave, Duke called out, "Coco, wait!"

She stopped. "Yes?"

"Listen, I know what happened in the lunchroom today was . . . embarrassing," he began. "But it kind of hurt my feelings when you went to sit with Mandy and Randy."

"But my lunch . . . eet was squashed," Coco said.

"I know, but Nova had soup to share," Duke pointed out. "And also, it looked like you were laughing at us."

Coco grinned. "Well, it *was* funny when you jumped on the table," she said.

"I only did that because I'm afraid of frogs, and Mandy and Randy know it," Duke said. "I'm pretty sure they're the ones who put that frog under our table in the first place—to scare me."

Coco frowned. "That eez very mean. Would they really do something like that?"

Duke frowned. "Well, I don't have any proof . . ."

Coco took a breath. "Duke, I must confess something," she said. "I was very scared to come here to Barksdale. I was afraid I would not fit in."

"My friends and I definitely don't fit in, either," Duke pointed out. "But we're nice. And we have fun together."

"Yes, you are all very nice," Coco agreed. "But I also fit in with Mandy and Randy. They are on my team for the—what eez it?—Field Day? So we will need to practice together anyway."

"I guess," Duke said. "But you can still sit with us at lunch."

"I am sorry, Duke, but we are going to come up with a practice plan tomorrow," she said. "This Field Day eez a very big deal. There is zee school spirit challenge, and zee brain activities . . ."

FIELD DAY
MATHALON

"Brain activities?" Duke asked. "There are no brain activities. Field Day has games and races. Running around and stuff."

Duke saw a flicker of worry in Coco's eyes, but he wasn't sure why. *Is she worried the Underdogs will embarrass her by messing up the challenges?*

"Oh, really?" she said. "How interesting. Now, I do not want to keep Auntie waiting."

Coco left, and Duke gave Mr. Quacky a hug.

"I think Peanut's right, Mr. Quacky," Duke said sadly. "Coco is too cool to be our friend."

CHAPTER 8

GIVE ME A "B"!

"All right, Underdogs, it's time to practice for our next challenge!" Nova announced the next day after school.

Duke, Peanut, and Harley had all gathered in Nova's backyard to work on their school spirit challenge for Field Day.

"Let's warm up with some laps around the house!" Nova suggested, and she took off running, with Harley and Peanut at her heels. Duke just sighed and sat down in the grass.

Nova stopped and looked back at Duke. "Come on, Duke! It's warm-up time!"

"What's the point?" Duke asked.

"The point is, we want to pass the loyalty challenge," Nova said. "We passed the first test, didn't we? Let's keep the momentum going!"

Duke moaned and lay back. "You don't get it! Why are we trying? So we can fit in? So we can impress meanies like Mandy and Randy?"

Harley and Peanut looked at Nova. They hadn't really thought about it like that before.

"Well, I'm not doing it for anyone else but *me*," Nova replied. "I want to be the best Nova that I can be. And to be my best, I have to at least *try* my best. So if warming up is not right for you, don't sweat it."

"Actually, we'll be the ones sweating it," Peanut mumbled, and the three dogs took off running around the house.

Duke stayed and stared at the Barksdale sky. It was perfectly blue, the color of a robin's egg, and clouds that looked like cotton-ball puffs floated in the air.

Barksdale even has the best sky, Duke thought. *What is a weird scaredy-dog like me doing here, anyway?*

After five laps around the house, Nova and Peanut stopped in front of Duke, panting. Harley kept going.

"Just one more. **WHOOPEE!**"

Harley ran around the house three more times before she finally stopped.

"Okay, Nova, what's next?" she asked eagerly.

Nova picked up a clipboard. "Well, we all know that the best way to show school spirit is with a cheer," she replied. "I asked everyone to come with an idea. Who wants—"

Peanut waved his paw. "Oooh, me, me, me!"

"Let's hear it, Peanut," Nova said.

Peanut cleared his throat.

BARKSDALE, BARKSDALE, can't be beat! We've all got the stinkiest feet!

Nova, Harley, and Duke stared at Peanut.

"Um, I like the rhyme, Peanut, but what do stinky feet have to do with school spirit?" Nova asked.

Peanut shrugged. "Nothing, but it's funny."

Nova looked at Harley. "What did you come up with?"

"Check this out!" Harley said, and then she began to sing.

BARKSDALE ACADEMY IS REALLY GREAT! The DESKS ARE NICE AND THERE ARE LOTS OF SQUIRRELS OUTSIDE AND I LOVE it WHEN it'S PEANUT butteR cookie DAY AND OH YEAH the teacheRS ARE PRETTY COOL, too!

"Whoa, nice, Harley!" Peanut said.

Nova nodded. "Yes, lots of great stuff in there, Harley, except it doesn't rhyme like a cheer should."

She turned to Duke. "Did you come up with anything?"

Duke sighed. "Um, sure."

Rah, rah, Barksdale.
Go, Barksdale. Yeah.

His voice sounded flat and bored.

"Hmm, well, that could maybe use some more pep," Nova said. "Here's the one I came up with:

Barksdale, Barksdale, is the best!
Barksdale's better than the rest!

"Give me a *B!* Give me an *A!* Give me an *R!* Give me a *K!* Give me an *S!* . . ."

Peanut started to make loud snoring sounds while Nova chanted and chanted.

". . . Give me an *L!* Give me an *E!* Give me an *A!* . . ."

Duke actually *did* doze off. He woke up just as Nova finished, and he wiped the drool from his chin.

". . . Give me a *D!* Give me a *Y!* What's that spell?"

"You can't spell out 'Barksdale Academy.' That will take too long!" Peanut cried.

Nova sighed. "I guess you're right. We can keep working on the cheer at our next practice. We also need a routine to show our school spirit, too. My sister Nina was head cheerleader when she was in school, and she said making a pyramid always impresses the judges."

"You want us to build a pyramid? What, out of big rocks?" Peanut asked.

Nova shook her shaggy head. "No, I mean we use our bodies to make a doggy pyramid. With me and Duke on the bottom, and then Harley stands on top of us, and then Peanut climbs to the very top."

"Hmm," Duke said. "That doesn't sound too bad. Just as long as I definitely get to be on the bottom."

"Dude, you would totally squash us if you were on the top," Peanut pointed out.

Nova walked out to a big patch of grass and planted her front legs on the ground, keeping her back flat.

"Duke, come next to me and do the same thing," she instructed.

Duke got into position next to Nova.

"Harley—" Nova began, but Harley was already running toward them.

"I got this!" she said. **"HERE I COME!"**

She jumped onto Nova and Duke, planting two legs on Nova and two on Duke.

Duke started to giggle. "Harley, that tickles!"

"I'm not doing anything. I'm just standing here," she protested.

Duke's back moved up and down as he laughed. "I can't help it. It tickles!"

"Hold still, Duke," Nova said. "Peanut, you need to climb up onto Duke's back and then jump onto Harley's back."

Peanut looked up at Harley. "It's high, but I think I can do it," he said. He jumped onto Duke.

Duke giggled again. "Now *you're* tickling me!"

"Knock it off, Duke!" Peanut said. "I'm losing my balance!"

But Duke couldn't help it. He giggled harder. And harder. His body shook.

Peanut jumped up on Harley's back.

"I did it!" he cried. "But, Duke, stop laughing! You're shaking the whole pyramid! I'm going to—"

Harley and Peanut tumbled off Nova and Duke. Still shaking with laughter, Duke bumped into Nova, knocking her down, too.

The four pups giggled, scrambling to their feet.

"Sorry," Duke said. "I didn't know I was so ticklish!"

Harley grinned. "It's okay, that was fun!"

Peanut shook his head. "Yeah, but I don't think this is gonna work for Field Day."

"Maybe not," Nova said. "But don't worry, Underdogs! We're going to get this right in time for the K-2 exam!"

"How are we going to do that?" Duke asked.

Nova grinned. "Remember what we learned in the agility challenge? We're going to do things the Underdog way!"

104

CHAPTER 9

ALL FUN AND GAMES?

"**T**he Underdog way? Don't you mean the *loser* way?"

The Underdogs turned to see Mandy, Randy, and Coco on the sidewalk next to Nova's yard.

"We're not losers!" Harley shot back.

"Yeah, we passed our first exam this year!" Nova added.

"But you got the lowest score," Mandy pointed out. "Which makes you losers."

"Yeah, with a capital 'L,'" Randy said, chuckling.

Coco, Duke noticed, was gazing at a bird in a tree.

Why won't she stick up for us? he wondered, and it made him feel sad.

Peanut marched up to Mandy and Randy. "Don't you have anything better to do than watch us practice? Shouldn't *you* be practicing your own cheer?"

"Don't worry about *us*," Mandy replied. "We've got something planned that's going to be the absolute best."

"Right, the best!" Randy echoed.

Mandy looked at Coco. *"Right,* Coco?"

"Er, yes, right," Coco replied, avoiding the gaze of the Underdogs.

Then Mandy and Randy lifted their snouts in the air and trotted away, with Coco at their heels.

Duke ran after her.

His cousin stopped. Mandy and Randy looked back and glared at her.

"I will just be one minute," Coco said. "What eez it, Duke?"

"Why didn't you say anything back there?" he asked. "Do you really think my friends and I are losers?"

"Of course not," she replied. "You are very nice. But eet is all fun and games, is eet not?"

Duke frowned. "I don't think name-calling is very fun."

"Field Day will be over soon," Coco said. "And then we will hang out again, Cousin. Okay?"

"Okay," Duke agreed with a sigh.

He walked back to his friends.

"Don't let Coco bother you, Duke," Nova said. "She's new here, and she's just trying to fit in with her team."

"That's what she said," Duke replied. "But it still hurts my feelings."

Peanut slapped him on the back. "You've got us, dude! Now, what were we doing before those fur-brains interrupted us?"

"We were trying to come up with a school spirit routine," Nova replied.

"Trying—and looking ridiculous," Duke said.

Nova grinned. "Don't worry. Nobody is going to make fun of us on Field Day. I've got a plan!"

CHAPTER 10

BOWWOW, BARKSDALE!

The sky above the Barksdale Academy competition field was the perfect shade of blue on the morning of Field Day.

All the students from Barksdale sat on one half of the bleachers. The pups from Pawston School for Canine Excellence sat on the other half.

Duke got a little nervous when he saw the polished group of Pawston pups. But they all looked a little nervous, too.

111

Then it hit Duke. *They've never won a Field Day against Barksdale! I guess the Pawston pups are underdogs, too, just like us!* he realized.

Duke quickly relaxed as the Field Day festivities began. First, each Barksdale team performed their school cheer, starting with the first-year students. Groups of adorable little puppies tumbled and jumped on the field, and the older pups clapped and cheered. Over at the judges' table, Principal Finefur and Coach Houndstooth scribbled down scores.

"When do we find out if we pass the K-2 loyalty test or not?" Duke asked Nova.

"Remember last year? The judges will add up our scores for school spirit and overall performance after the event is over. If our total score is more than sixty-five, we'll pass," Nova explained.

Then Principal Finefur's voice came through the speakers. "And now it's time for the year-four students to show us some school spirit. First up—Team Underdog!"

Duke, Nova, Peanut, and Harley stood up. They piled their paws on top of one another and cheered together. **"GO, UNDERDOGS!"**

Duke felt pretty confident as they walked out onto the field and faced the bleachers. Nova's granny had made them special pom-poms to wave during their performance. They had come up with a new cheer and a new routine, and they had been practicing it all week.

Harley, Duke, Nova, and Peanut lined up on the field.

"Ready, Underdogs?" Nova called out.
"READY!" Harley, Duke, and Peanut shouted back.
Then they launched into their cheer.

Bowwow, Barksdale can't be beat!
We've got great teachers and furry feet!
Bowwow, Barksdale is the best!
Our squirrels are faster
than all the rest!

Then Duke, Nova, and Peanut got down on the ground. Harley hurried down the field and then began running toward the three dogs. Duke squeezed his eyes shut. He knew what was coming, but he was too afraid to watch.

Right before she got to them, Harley launched into the air. She soared over Nova, over Duke, over . . .

OUCH!

Well, she almost soared over Peanut. Instead, she landed on him, squashing him. Everyone in the stands laughed.

"Don't give up, guys!" Nova called out. "It's our big finish!"

Peanut shook himself off and jumped to his feet. The four dogs held paws.

"GO, BARKSDALE!" they yelled.

Duke's heart was pounding as they ran back to the bleachers.

"Sorry, pups," Harley said. "Especially you, Peanut."

"It's okay," Peanut said. "You almost made it."

"I think we did pretty good," Nova said. "We were loud, and we didn't mess up our cheer. I feel good about this!"

They sat in the bleachers and watched the other year-four teams perform their cheers.

Athena's team brought a table with test tubes onto the field and mixed chemicals to make puffy clouds of blue and yellow—the Barksdale colors.

Another team made a pyramid. And another used blue-and-yellow ribbons to deliver their rhyming cheer.

"Rah, rah, Barksdale, we're the best!
So much better than all the rest!"

Peanut whispered to Duke. "I think our cheer was better."

"Yeah," Duke agreed. "Compared to everyone else, I think we did okay."

"And finally, let's see what Team Awesome has to offer!" Principal Finefur announced.

Everyone cheered and looked for Mandy, Randy, Ollie, and Coco to come down from the stands. But that didn't happen. Instead . . .

BAM! A huge cloud of blue smoke appeared on the field, and the four pups emerged from it as if by magic. They were all wearing shirts covered in shiny blue and gold sequins, and Ollie was holding an electric guitar. He played a chord, and then Team Awesome began to sing.

The crowd in the bleachers answered back. **"WIN!"**
"Barksdale!"
"WIN!"
"B-B-B-B-B-B-Barksdale ROCKS!" Team
Awesome finished, and then fireworks lit up
behind them.

Every dog in the stands jumped to their feet—even the Underdogs.

"Wow, that was amazing!" Nova said.

On the field, Coco was grinning, and Duke felt happy for his cousin. But a thought worried him.

After today, Coco's going to be more popular than ever, he thought. *She's never going to want to hang out with me again!*

CHAPTER 11

TRIPPING AND SLIPPING

"And now it's time for the games to begin!" Principal Finefur announced to the crowd. "Each class of students will compete in a set of three challenges. The winning team in each challenge earns a point for their school. Principal Howler and Coach Curlytail from Pawston will join me and Coach Houndstooth at the judges' table."

Duke settled into his seat on the bleachers to watch the Barksdale teams compete. The first-year challenges were the simplest: a beanbag toss, a baton relay, and a tail-wagging contest. The Barksdale puppies won the toss and the relay, and lost the tail-wagging contest when a Pawston poodle wagged her tail the longest. The scoreboard read:

"Bowwow, Barksdale!" Nova cheered, and everyone clapped as the first-year students left the field.

The Barksdale second-year students won the sack race and the beach ball toss but lost the barking contest when a Pawston bulldog barked the loudest.

"Bowwow, Barksdale! Barksdale is the best!" the Barksdale students cheered.

A team of Barksdale third-year students wove around orange cones to win the speed relay, and another Barksdale team filled a can with balls the fastest to earn another point. But a Pawston team beat everyone to the finish line in the wheelbarrow race.

"Barksdale is doing great!" Nova remarked as the fourth-year students made their way onto the field. "It looks like we're going to win for the fifty-fourth year in a row. I kind of feel bad for Pawston."

"Me too," Duke agreed. "I just hope Team Underdog doesn't mess things up too much. We didn't do so well when we practiced the challenges in your backyard."

Nova grinned. "We just have to try our best, and I'm sure we'll get enough points to pass. Let's stay focused and remember what we practiced!"

Duke gazed over at Team Awesome. They all strode confidently onto the field. Then he blinked. Coco didn't look as confident as the others. In fact, his cousin looked kind of nervous.

That's weird, he thought. *What does Coco have to be nervous about?*

"Our first challenge is an egg race," Professor Finefur announced. "The first team to reach the finish line without breaking their egg will win a point for their school."

The pups took their places for the challenge. Rows of four cones were lined up from one end of the field to the other—one row for each team. In the Underdogs' row, Peanut stood by the first cone, Duke stood by the second, Nova by the third, and Harley by the fourth. In his mouth, Peanut carefully held a spoon with an egg resting on it.

"ON YOUR BARK, GET SET, GO!"

Peanut slowly walked across the grass to bring the egg to Duke. To his left and right, Duke could see other dogs moving faster, but he tried not to worry about that. He just focused on Peanut.

"If we take it slowly, we won't drop the egg," Nova had said during practice.

Peanut reached Duke and gently transferred the egg to the spoon in his mouth. Duke took a deep breath and made his way toward Nova. She eagerly wagged her tail, waiting for him, but she refrained from cheering him on. In practice, that had spooked him and he'd dropped the egg.

Duke reached Nova and dropped the egg into her spoon. She walked toward Harley, and Duke looked back at the other teams. Two of the Barksdale teams had already dropped their eggs and were out! But Ollie on Team Awesome was zipping toward Coco. And on the Pawston side, three teams were still in the race.

Nova reached Harley. Harley spit out the spoon in her mouth . . . and gobbled down the egg!

Then her eyes got wide with horror as she realized what she'd done.

"Oh no!" she cried. "I . . . I saw the egg and my brain yelled **'EAT!'** and . . ."

"It's okay," Nova told her. "Look, Coco's on her way to the finish line. Team Awesome's gonna win this for Barksdale!"

Coco hurried toward the finish line, three steps ahead of a spotted Pawston pup.

"Go, Team Awesome!" the crowd cheered.

Then Coco tripped! The egg flew out of her spoon. It somersaulted through the air.

It landed on top of Coach Houndstooth's head and cracked!

The crowd gasped. Coco looked down at her feet. And the spotted Pawston pup crossed the finish line.

"The point goes to Pawston!" Principal Finefur announced. "And does anyone have a washcloth for Coach Houndstooth?"

CHAPTER 12

SPLASHING AND CRASHING

Mandy and Randy ran up to Coco.

"What happened?" Mandy asked.

"Yeah, what happened?" Randy repeated.

Coco shrugged. "There must have been a rock on zee track."

"Well, be more careful next time!" Mandy snapped.

"Yeah, more careful!" Randy added.

133

Coco looked sad, and Duke felt bad for her.

Can't Mandy and Randy ever be nice? he wondered.

"The next challenge is the six-legged race!" Principal Finefur announced.

The Underdogs had practiced for this one, too. The team members lined up. Peanut's left legs were tied to Duke's right legs. Nova tied her right legs to Harley's left legs.

Duke gazed over at Team Awesome. Mandy and Randy were tied together, and Coco was tied to Ollie. Duke remembered that Ollie and super-fast

Ace had always teamed up together on Field Day, and he wondered if Coco was just as fast, too.

Why wouldn't she be? he thought. *She's so good at everything else . . . Except maybe that egg toss . . .*

"On your bark, get set, go!"

The teams took off, racing across the field. Nova and Harley sped ahead quickly. Peanut lifted up his two left paws and let Duke carry him down the field. Peanut had tried leaving his paws down during practice, but there was no way his tiny legs could keep up with Duke's meaty ones.

"Peanut, put those paws on the ground or you'll be disqualified!" Principal Finefur yelled, and Peanut obeyed.

Duke slowed way down.

Nearby, Mandy and Randy were arguing.

"Left paws first!" Mandy yelled.

"I am moving my left paws!" Randy protested.

"No, I mean, *my* left paws first, and *your* right paws!" Mandy shouted.

Randy stopped. **"I AM SO CONFUSED!"**

The Pawston teams raced ahead of all the Barksdale teams except for one: Ollie and Coco. Powered by Ollie's back wheels, they sped ahead of all the other dogs.

"Go, Barksdale! Go, Team Awesome!" the crowd cheered.

But then . . . Coco tripped! She and Ollie flipped over and skidded across the field on Ollie's wheels.

Bam! They knocked into the Powerpup beverage stand.

Splash! The bright blue liquid rained down on them.

A team from Pawston hopped over the finish line, and everyone gasped. And then they began to talk with loud whispers.

"What's wrong with Coco?"

"Isn't she supposed to be the best student in France?"

"I thought Coco was supposed to be cool, but she's so clumsy . . ."

Coco looked down at the ground, and Duke knew she heard the comments, too.

Then he remembered something. He remembered how Coco had looked nervous at the start of the games. And how she had looked nervous when Duke told her the challenges were physical ones, not brain games.

Whoa! he realized. *Coco is an Underdog, too!*

CHAPTER 13

SPLAT!

The year-four students had only one more challenge left, and Barksdale Academy was quickly losing its lead.

But Duke wasn't paying attention to the score. He was staring at his cousin.

Poor Coco, he thought. *I know what it feels like to be the center of attention for the wrong reason!*

Then Peanut tapped him. "Hey, dude, we have to get ready for the water balloon toss," he said.

"Oh yeah," Duke replied, and he followed Peanut to Nova and Harley, who were high-fiving.

"Did you see that? Harley and I crossed the finish line in third place!" Nova announced.

"Wow, that's great!" Duke said.

"It was easy," Nova explained. "Harley and I are besties. We know how to move together."

Harley nodded. "It felt great to do a good job in that race," she said, but her furry eyebrows furrowed. "Maybe now everyone will forget about me eating that egg. I'm sure we'll lose points for *that* when we get graded for overall performance!"

"We're going to pass the K-2 exam," Nova assured her. "I just know it! We haven't messed up anything *really* bad, like we have in the past."

"Yeah, like that year you ate a whole bucket of tennis balls," Peanut said. "At least this year it was only one egg."

Harley brightened. "Yeah, that's true!"

Then Principal Finefur's voice came over the speakers. "All right, everybody, you know how this works," she said. "Pair up with one of your teammates and take one water balloon. Then stand across from each other at the cones. At the sound of the whistle, toss the balloon to your partner. If you break the balloon, you're out. The team that can toss the balloon back and forth the most times without breaking it will earn one point for their school."

Duke picked up a balloon and faced Peanut. Nova and Harley lined up on Duke's left, and Coco and Ollie were to Duke's right.

Duke looked over at his cousin. "You got this, Coco," he said, and she smiled weakly at him. But Duke could see that her ears were drooping.

Coach Houndstooth blew his whistle.

TWEET!

Duke tossed the balloon to Peanut, and he caught it. Coco tossed the balloon to Ollie, and he caught it.

TWEET!

Peanut tossed the balloon to Duke, but the toss was low. Duke reached down . . . but he couldn't grab it in time.

SPLAT! The balloon broke. Next to him, Ollie's water balloon soared toward Coco. She stared at it, her eyes wide with fear. When it neared her, she flailed her paws wildly. The balloon soared to her left.

SPLAT! It landed on Mandy's head, just as she was trying to catch the balloon Randy tossed her.

SPLAT! Randy's balloon splashed on Mandy, too. She turned to Coco, her eyes blazing.

"Coco, what is the matter with you? I thought it would be great to have you on our team, but you can't do anything right!"

Coco's eyes filled with tears.

"I . . . I am not good at zeez kind of games," she said.

"No, you're not!" Mandy agreed. "In fact, you're terrible!"

TWEET!

Nova caught the balloon that Harley tossed to her. Then she marched over to Mandy.

"Don't be so mean, Mandy. Anybody could drop a water balloon. See?" Nova said, slamming her water balloon onto the ground.

SPLAT! It splashed all over her and Mandy, whose fur was now even more drenched.

"That's not funny, Nova!" Mandy fumed.

Peanut ran to the basket of water balloons and picked up one in each paw.

WATER BALLOON FIGHT!

Peanut threw one balloon at Randy and one at Harley.

"Hey!" Randy yelled, but Harley grinned.

"Yeah!" She ran and got more water balloons, and some of the other Barksdale pups started throwing water balloons at one another, too.

TWEET! TWEET! TWEET! Coach Houndstooth kept blowing the whistle.

"Students! Stop this right now!" Principal Finefur yelled over the megaphone. "We are going to take points away from your loyalty test scores!"

That threat calmed everyone down. The last water balloons landed in the grass with a splat. Duke watched Coco slowly walk away and slump down on the bleachers.

TWEET!

"All the Barksdale teams are disqualified!" Principal Finefur announced. "Pawston gets the point!"

Duke looked at the scoreboard.

The fourth-year class had lost Barksdale's lead! Soggy and sorry, the students slowly returned to the stands.

The year-five students went next, and then the year-six students. But something happened to the Pawston pups after sweeping the year-four contests. They didn't look nervous anymore. They looked confident. They won the bone-burying challenge, and the howling hoedown, and the tug-of-war, and the sack race. And in the end the score was . . .

The Barksdale students stared at the score in disbelief. So did the Pawston pups. Then the Pawston students burst into cheers and started hugging one another and jumping up and down.

Duke couldn't help smiling. He felt happy for Pawston. *It must feel nice to win after being underdogs for so long*, he thought.

But gloom fell over the Barksdale bleachers. "This can't be happening!" someone wailed. "Barksdale has never lost to Pawston!"

Then Mandy stood up. "I blame Coco," she said, pointing. "It's all *her* fault!"

CHaPTeR 14

LOYALTY

"**W**e were in the lead until Coco the klutz started messing things up," Mandy said loudly.

Some of the pups giggled.

"Coco the klutz!" Randy repeated.

Other pups joined in. "Coco the klutz! Coco the klutz! Coco the klutz!"

Tears started to fall down Coco's furry cheeks.

"Students, stop this right now!" Principal Finefur said into the microphone.

Duke felt sad for his cousin. Then he felt angry.

EVERYBODY, JUST STOP IT!

The pups all got quiet and stared at Duke. His heart began to beat fast, but he kept going. "Please leave my cousin Coco alone. So what if she's a little clumsy? She's smart and funny and is good at a lot of other things. Nobody's good at everything, right? A lot of us could have done better today. Pawston won fair and square, and it's not right to blame Coco."

Everyone got quiet.

"Are you finished, Duke?" Principal Finefur asked.

He nodded. "I'm—I don't know what came over me. But Coco is my cousin, and I—"

"That's enough, Duke," she said, and Duke's heart sank. The Underdogs had messed up some of the challenges. Then they'd sort of accidentally started a water balloon fight. And now he'd interrupted Principal Finefur. Would she take even *more* points off their loyalty test grade because of what Duke had just done?

"If we fail because of me, I'm sorry," he whispered to his friends.

"It's okay, Duke," Peanut replied. "I don't care if we fail. You did the right thing!"

Nova and Harley nodded in agreement.

"It's time for the closing ceremonies!" Principal Finefur announced.

Principal Finefur and Coach Houndstooth handed over the Field Day trophy to Principal Howler and Coach Curlytail of the Pawston School. The Barksdale students clapped politely.

Then Nova yelled out, "Three cheers for Pawston!"
The Underdogs all joined in the cheer with Nova,
along with some of the other Barksdale students.

The Pawston students and staff climbed aboard their bus. Then Principal Finefur picked up her clipboard and spoke into the microphone.

"We had a disappointing loss to Pawston today," she began. "But let me be clear, students—there is no one pup responsible for this loss. We failed as a school."

Mandy and Randy gasped.

"But some of us won challenges!" Mandy protested.

"Perhaps, but we all lost when we began to turn on our teammates," Principal Finefur scolded. "We shouldn't be sad, though. We didn't win this year. But there's always next year!"

The Barksdale pups cheered up at that, and some of them clapped.

"Now then, the results of this year's loyalty test," she said. "There were many wonderful displays of school spirit today, and so many of you did your best in the challenges. Even though our school lost against Pawston, your loyalty to Barksdale was excellent. I shall read the scores, starting with year one."

The Underdogs held paws as the scores were announced. Most teams passed with scores of 90 or higher.

"Team Awesome, your school spirit was the best we've seen in years," Principal Finefur said. "And for the most part, you did well in the challenges. But Coach Houndstooth and I must take off points for you, Mandy and Randy, for poor sportsmanship against one of your own teammates. Your final score is eighty-eight."

Mandy and Randy scowled but didn't argue.

"Now for Team Underdog," Principal Finefur said, and the four pups sat up a little straighter. "We enjoyed your school spirit display, although you lost a few points due to the rough ending. And we had to deduct twenty points for starting a water balloon fight—"

Peanut looked up at the sky, and Duke flinched. *Is she going to take points off for my speech, too? Did we fail again?*

"—but the way you all stuck up for Duke's cousin showed real loyalty, which is what this challenge is all about. You pass with a score of seventy-seven."

Nova shrieked, and the four Underdogs hugged.

Principal Finefur read off the rest of the scores, and then the pups gathered on the field for snacks and bowls of bright blue Powerpup beverage. Coco walked up to the Underdogs.

"Hey, Coco, why didn't you tell us you were a klutz?" Peanut asked, and Duke nudged him.

Coco laughed. "That's okay. I am very clumsy, eet is true. At my school, eet is not a big deal. We are focused on books and style and poise. I am very good at all those things. I was not expecting zee Field Day activities to be so physical."

Then she took a deep breath and looked at Duke right in the eyes. "Cousin, I owe you and your friends a big apology," she said. "I was so worried about fitting in that I did not stand up to Mandy and Randy when they were not being nice. I am very sorry."

"Thanks," Duke replied. "I know it couldn't have been easy, coming here to a new school."

"I am so used to being very popular back home," Coco admitted. "I was afraid of what it would feel like if I was not popular here. But that is not a good excuse. You and your friends . . . you stuck up for me when I did not stick up for you."

"That's the Underdog way," Duke replied.

"Well, I would rather be like you than like Mandy and Randy," Coco said. "Can I seet with you at lunch again?"